MC VEGGIE FRESH ROCKS THE MIC

SHANON MORRIS, MS, RD, CDN
Illustrated by MERVE TERZI

First U.S. edition 2019

Library of Congress Catalog Card Number 2018908763

ISBN 97817325821-0-1 (Paperback Edition)

ISBN 978-1-7325821-1-8 (Hardback Edition)

Published in the United States of America

www.shanonmorris.com

To my niece, Rae. You are powerful, beautiful and unstoppable. Look, you already have a book dedicated to you and you can't even talk yet. Not bad. Not bad at all.

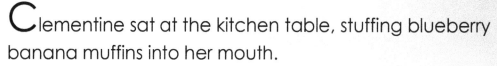

Clementine sat at the kitchen table, stuffing blueberry banana muffins into her mouth.

"Clementine! Clementine!

I know you can hear me over all of that loud chewing.

How many times have I told you to slow down when you eat?" said Clementine's mom.

"Sorry, Mom," Clementine mumbled as she took another bite.

Clementine loved everything about food: the way it looked and smelled, and of course, how it tasted. She knew a lot about healthy food because she helped her mom run the community garden near their apartment in Harlem.

"Today is the last day to sign up for the Healthy Hero Election. Are you going to sign up?" asked Clementine's mom. Clementine imagined herself giving a speech in front of the whole school.

"Ohhhhhhhhhh, a hero. SUPER CLEMENTINE IS HERE TO EAT ALL YOUR FOOOOOOD," sang her twin brothers, Sage and Basil.

Clementine gave her brothers a mean side-eye.
"I don't know if I have what it takes," she said.
"Ms. Healy said a Healthy Hero is a kid who is helpful, always plays in gym class and is a role model who makes good food choices."
"That sounds just like you," said Mom.
Clementine hugged her mom and sped out the front door.

All day, Clementine thought about what to do: during Mr. Jones' math lesson, upside down at recess, and even during lunch, her favorite time of day.

But when she got to Ms. Healy's class, she knew she had to decide.

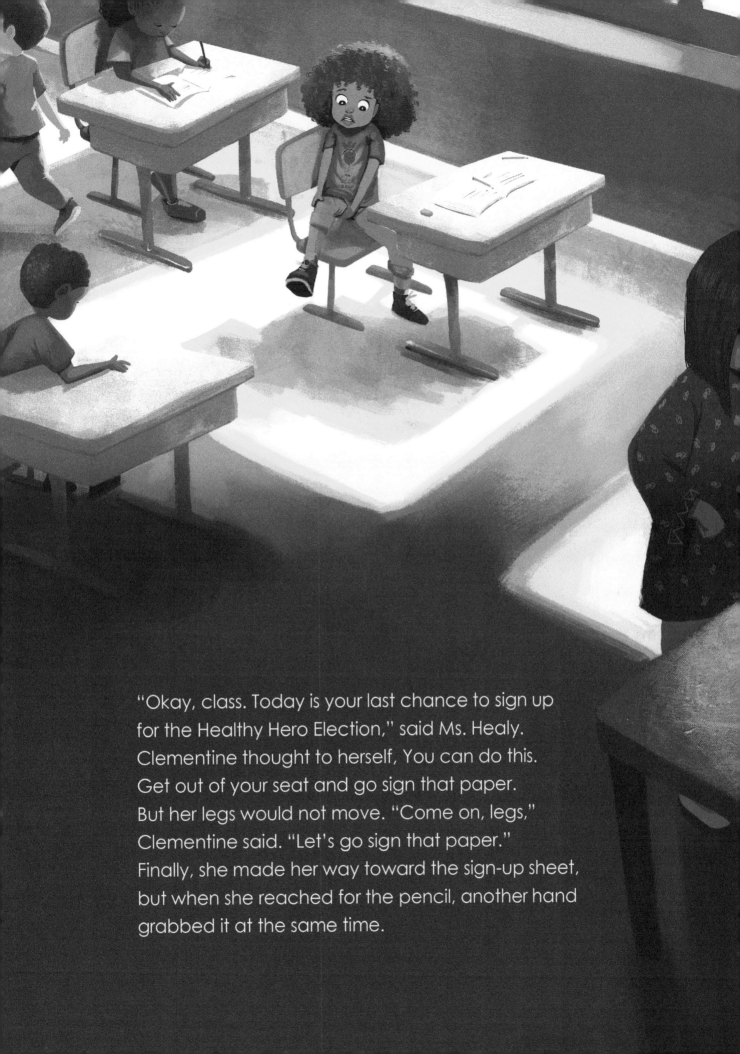

"Okay, class. Today is your last chance to sign up
for the Healthy Hero Election," said Ms. Healy.
Clementine thought to herself, You can do this.
Get out of your seat and go sign that paper.
But her legs would not move. "Come on, legs,"
Clementine said. "Let's go sign that paper."
Finally, she made her way toward the sign-up sheet,
but when she reached for the pencil, another hand
grabbed it at the same time.

"Hey! Let go! I had it first," said Edgar.
Edgar always made fun of Clementine's name and her
healthy lunches. Lots of kids at school called Edgar and
his friends "the Junk Food Friends" because they hung out
by the snack line in the cafeteria eating chips and candy,
and drinking soda.

"Ugh, what are you doing here?"
asked Clementine.
"Signing up for the election, duhhh,"
said Edgar as he grabbed the pencil.

"This isn't the Junk Food Hero Election.
It's the H-E-A-L-T-H-Y Hero election," Clementine spelled out.
"Who cares, all my Junk Food Friends will vote for me," said Edgar.

"But… but Edgar, do you even eat healthy food?" asked Clementine. Clementine remembered Edgar and his Junk Food Friends eating honey buns and drinking soda just this morning.

"No, but no one has to know that, Tangerine... I mean Orange, or is it little baby Clementine?" laughed Edgar.
"Yeahhhh, no one has to know," repeated his Junk Food Friends.
"My name is Clementine! Only someone who doesn't eat fruit wouldn't know the difference between a clementine, a tangerine and an orange!" yelled Clementine.

ORANGE

CLEMENTINE

TANGERINE

When the school bell rang, Clementine quickly put her name on the list and started to walk home.
I have to beat Edgar and his Junk Food Friends!
I'd better start working on my speech, thought Clementine.

When she got to her apartment, she went straight to her room and got to work. She looked in the mirror and said in a very serious voice, "Hi. My name is Clementine and I'm P.S. 23's Healthy Hero."

Clementine shook her head. "That sounds too boring."
She started again but in a bubbly voice.
"Hi everyone, I'm Clementine, your next Healthy He...."

She heard giggles outside her door. It had to be Basil and Sage. She wondered how long they'd been listening. Clementine opened her door.
"What do you guys want?"
Sage giggled. "Why are you talking so funny?"

"I'm practicing my Healthy Hero Speech for tomorrow,"
said Clementine.
"What's a healthy hero again?" asked Basil.
"It's someone who loves to help people be healthy. Kinda
like how mom helps us eat food to feel good every day.
She's our healthy hero," explained Clementine.

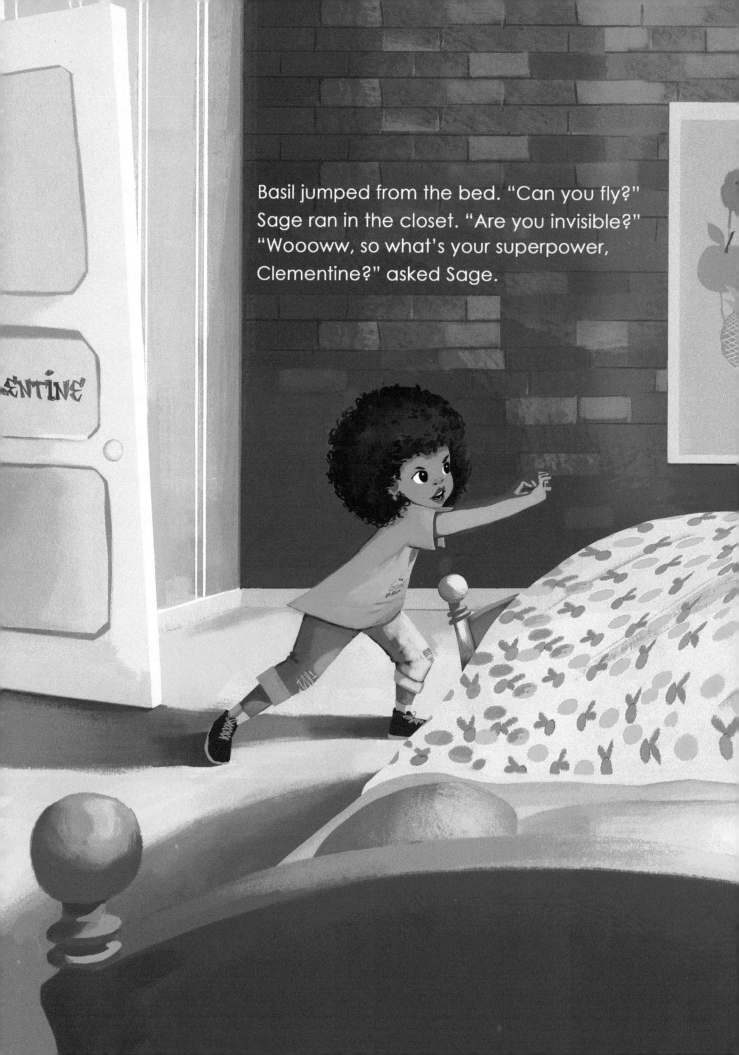

Basil jumped from the bed. "Can you fly?"
Sage ran in the closet. "Are you invisible?"
"Woooww, so what's your superpower,
Clementine?" asked Sage.

"Noooo. I just umm ... I don't know yet,"
Clementine replied. Basil ran to the mirror and
started making fun of Clementine.
"Hi I'm Clemy! I'm a veggie hero and my superpower
is I can eat twenty cranberry minis all by myself".
Clementine tried to catch her brothers as they ran
around her room.

"Mommmmmmmmmm, tell them to stop bothering me!" screamed Clementine.

"Basil…Sage, come help me cook dinner!
I need your help mixing, measuring and taste testing!"
yelled Mom.
Basil and Sage ran down to the kitchen.

Finally, Clementine was able to focus.

I promise to be the best Healthy Hero ever. I will high five anyone I see with a piece of fruit at lunch, Clementine wrote.

No, that isn't any good. Before she knew it, her room was full of crumbled papers, each piece with a different bad idea.

"Hey, baby girl, you look like you're having some trouble,"
said Mom.
"Yeah, I am."
Clementine climbed over the mountain of bad ideas.
"I don't know what to say."
"Just be yourself and it will all be fine," said Mom.

Clementine wanted to believe her mom, but she wasn't sure. As she fell asleep that night, she heard loud music coming from outside her window. She hopped out of bed and saw a group of people freestyle rapping on the stoop across the street.

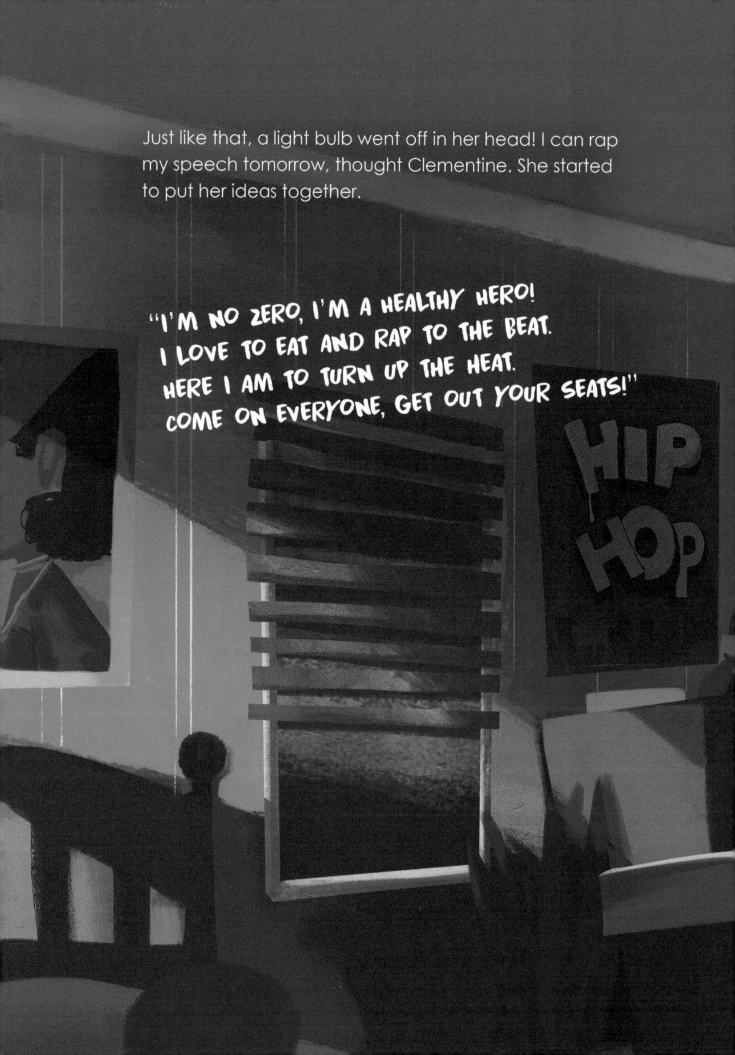

Just like that, a light bulb went off in her head! I can rap my speech tomorrow, thought Clementine. She started to put her ideas together.

"I'M NO ZERO, I'M A HEALTHY HERO!
I LOVE TO EAT AND RAP TO THE BEAT.
HERE I AM TO TURN UP THE HEAT.
COME ON EVERYONE, GET OUT YOUR SEATS!"

Clementine stayed up late working on her Healthy Hero rap. She couldn't wait for the whole school to hear it at the election.

The next day, Clementine walked into the school auditorium feeling like a Healthy Hero. She sat behind the stage as she waited her turn to give her speech. First up was Soccer Sasha, who bounced a soccer ball on her head and promised to teach everyone how to do it. The kids were amazed.

Second up was Farmer's Market Frank. His family sold homemade jam at the farmer's market on 125th Street. Frank promised to give everyone a jar of jam if they voted for him. Clementine thought, If I weren't running I'd vote for him. Who doesn't looove jam?

Next up was Edgar, who was all dressed up in a fancy suit. "If you vote for me, me and my friends will be the school's Junk Food Patrol," he said. Someone from the crowd yelled, "What does the Junk Food Patrol do?"
"We'll take all of your unhealthy snacks from you," said Edgar, smiling from ear to ear.

"And what will you do with the unhealthy snacks?" asked Ms. Healy.
"We'll throw them away," said Edgar. But his Junk Food Friends said,
"No, we won't! Edgar, you said we can take the snacks
and eat them."
Everyone started to boo. "Booooooooooooooooooooooooo!"
Edgar and his Junk Food Friends ran off the stage.

Clementine knew this was her chance to beat Edgar and his Junk Food Friends.
"Are you ready? You're up next!" said Ms. Healy.
Clementine peeked through the curtain and saw her mom setting up her favorite salsa with whole grain tortilla chips and remembered what she had said about being yourself.
"Yes, I'm ready, Ms. Healy," said Clementine.
"Okay, well, show them what you've got!"

Clementine jumped up, grabbed the microphone,
and took the stage.
"Hi, my name is MC Veggie Fresh," said Clementine.
She put on a pair of sunglasses and pulled her
mother's gold chain out of her shirt.

"I SPIT HEALTHY RHYMES,
BY RHYMING WHAT I SPIT
TO HELP ALL THE KIDS
GET WHAT I GET."

"YOU ARE WHAT YOU EAT,
BUT YOU GOTTA THINK ON YOUR FEET,
IT'S EASY TO BE TRICKED,
SO BE CAREFUL WITH YOUR TREATS
EATING HEALTHY IS WHAT WE SHOULD DO."

"WHO DOESN'T LOVE TO CHEW, CHEW, CHEW—
GREENS, REDS, YELLOWS, AND BLUES,
ALL IN OUR TUMMIES,
NO NEED FOR THOSE GUMMIES!"

"FROM THE START OF THE DAY,
LET'S PLAY, PLAY, PLAY.
FOLLOW ME AND I'LL LEAD THE WAY.
I'M YOUR HEALTHY HERO—
MC VEGGIE FRESH SAVES THE DAY!"

WHEN I SAY "VEGGIE," YOU SAY "FRESH."
"VEGGIE!"
"FRESH!"
"VEGGIE!"
"FRESH!"

When her rap was over, everyone jumped to their feet and clapped for MC Veggie Fresh—even Edgar and his Junk Food Friends.

MC Veggie Fresh's rap helped her win the election. And as the new Healthy Hero at PS. 23 in Harlem, she helped everyone see how eating healthy can be fun! Soon, the whole school started helping out at the garden and asking for her Mom's delicious recipes.

RECIPES

🥦 Children who cook are more likely to have a healthy relationship with food as an adult, which allows them to make better food choices throughout their lives. If a child invests time and effort into the creation of their food, they are more likely to try the finished dish, and who knows, you might even have a little chef-in-training on your hands!

Before you get started, be sure to teach the rules of the kitchen:

🥦 **CLEAN YOUR HANDS:** before and after touching food make sure you wash your hands. Wash with soap and water for 20 seconds or sing the "ABCs" to make sure you get all those germs!

🥦 **SAFETY WITH KNIVES:** plastic knives or lettuce knives (knife with plastic serrated edge) are safe for children to use when cooking. But just because they are not very sharp doesn't mean you shouldn't follow the same knife safety rules as you would with a sharp knife. Sharper knives should be used by adults!

- The safest place for knives is facing away from you on the cutting board. If you must walk with a knife, keep the blade facing the ground, never wave in the air or point towards other people.
- Keep fingertips away from the knife blade. Try the bear claw method. With this technique, your hand is curled into a claw-like shape, with the fingernails holding the food.
- Use a rocking motion while cutting.

FOLLOW THE RECIPE: the recipe is your road map. It's best to read the recipe before you start so you know what lies ahead! If you don't follow it, you might get lost. Make sure you measure everything and read all details. It is easier with little helpers to prepare and measure out everything before combining and cooking, that way you don't miss a step.

DON'T YUCK MY YUM: children are easily influenced so it's important to not share negative opinions about food in front of them. Allow them to make their own opinions. Would you want to try a scary new food if your parent told you it was gross? Probably not.

CLEAN UP: make sure to clean up after yourself so the kitchen is ready for your next cooking session.

HAVE FUN!

Children are great mixers, mashers, choppers, cleaners, readers, tasters and leaders! They just have to be shown the right way. Look out for the highlighted steps that are perfect for your little chef to perform while making the recipe.

Remember, there are many healthy lessons to be learned in the kitchen. Have fun teaching and tasting them!

CRANBERRY MINIS

Servings: 20 minis

Ingredients
½ cup oats (steel cut oats, instant or gluten-free oats)
½ cup dried cranberries
1 cup unsweetened coconut flakes
¼ cup ground flaxseed
¼ cup honey
¾ cup sunbutter (any nut butter can be used)

Directions
- Mix together oats, cranberries, coconut and flaxseed in a mixing bowl.
- Add honey and sunbutter. Mix well until you have a sticky mixture.
- Scoop 2-3 tablespoons into your hand. Roll and press mixture into small balls.
- Refrigerate for 30 mins.
- Enjoy!

Notes:
- If your mixture is too wet add more oats or coconut flakes. If it's too dry, add honey or sunbutter.
- Any type of nutbutter can be used in the recipe like peanut or almond butter. Sunbutter is a yummy alternative for those kiddies with nut allergies.

CLEMENTINE'S SALSA

Servings: 8 servings

Ingredients
1 can black beans (15oz)
1 chopped avocado
3 clementines (oranges or tangerines)
1 cup chopped red onions
4 tablespoon chopped cilantro
3 limes
1 bag whole grain tortilla chips

Directions
- Rinse beans and pour into a bowl.
- Cut avocado in half and remove pit. Cut into small chunks and place inside bowl.
- Peel and dice clementines and onion. Add into bowl.
- Rinse the cilantro and dry in a paper towel. Remove the stems from cilantro and chop into small pieces. Add into the bowl.
- Cut limes in half or quarters and squeeze limes over salsa and mix.
- Serve with whole grain chips.
- Enjoy!

Note: If you don't like the taste of cilantro, try using parsley.

BLUEBERRY BANANA MUFFINS

Servings: 12 muffins

Ingredients

½ cup coconut flour
½ teaspoon baking soda
¼ teaspoon salt
4 eggs (room temperature)
¼ cup honey

¼ cup coconut oil (melted)
1 teaspoon vanilla extract
2 medium ripe bananas
⅔ cup frozen blueberries

Directions

- Preheat oven to 350 degrees.
- Grease muffin tin.
- In a bowl, mix together coconut flour, baking soda and salt.
- In a new bowl, mix the eggs, honey, coconut oil, and vanilla with a fork.
- Mash bananas and add to the wet mixture.
- Add the wet ingredients to the dry ingredients. Mix until well combined (don't over mix).
- Pour in blueberries and gently fold them into the mixture.
- Add mixture into each muffin cup. Add a small drop of honey to the top of each muffin (optional).
- Bake at 350 degrees for 20-25 mins.
- Let cool for 10-15 mins.
- Enjoy!

ABOUT THE AUTHOR

Shanon Morris is a Registered Dietitian who has been working with communities from children to senior citizens for the last decade with the goal of making nutrition education relatable, accessible and enjoyable for all. Shanon studied Nutrition at Howard University and Nutrition and Exercise Science at Columbia University. Those who know her might say Shanon lives to eat and they are probably right but when she isn't eating you can find her enjoying time with her family or traveling the world. Keep up with Shanon and MC Veggie Fresh at www.shanonmorris.com.

CPSIA information can be obtained
at www.ICGtesting.com
Printed in the USA
BVHW020610221220
595990BV00002BA/87

9 781732 58211